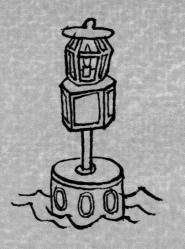

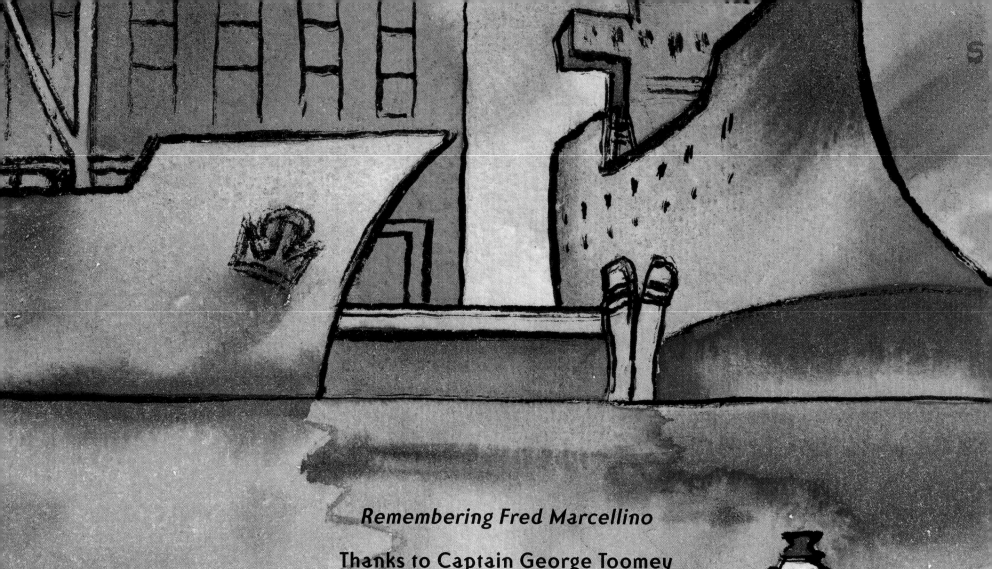

Remembering Fred Marcellino

**Thanks to Captain George Toomey
and Mike Hickey at Boston Towing
and Transportation**

We're MIGHTY grateful to
Justin Chanda, Joanna Cotler, Blair Dore, Holly McGhee,
Alicia Mikles, Jessica Shulsinger and Ruiko Tokunaga

5215 96/3

I'm Mighty! Text copyright © 2003 by Kate McMullan Illustrations copyright © 2003 by Jim McMullan Printed in the U.S.A. All rights reserved. www.harperchildrens.com Library of Congress Cataloging-in-Publication Data McMullan, Kate. I'm mighty! / Kate & Jim McMullan—1st ed. p. cm. Summary: A little tugboat shows how he can bring big ships into the harbor even though he is small. ISBN 0-06-009290-4 — ISBN 0-06-009291-2 (lib. bdg.) [1. Tugboats—Fiction. 2. Size—Fiction. 3. Ships—Fiction.] I. McMullan, Jim, 1936— , ill. II. Title. PZ7.M47879lm 2003 [E]—dc21 2002007948 Typography by Alicia Mikles 3 4 5 6 7 8 9 10 ❖ First Edition

ER DOOPER

GARRY KING II

TUGS

I'M MIGHTY!

KATE & JIM McMULLAN

JOANNA COTLER BOOKS

An Imprint of HarperCollinsPublishers

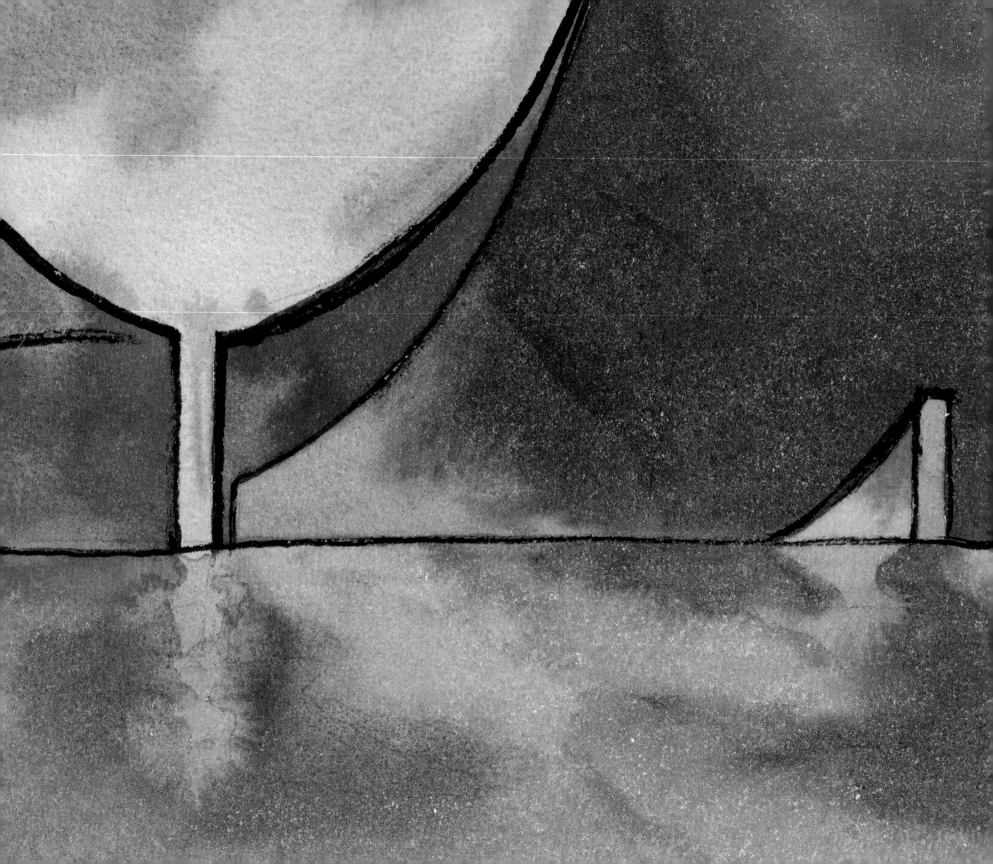

Hey!

Over here!

Yeah, me, the little guy.

When big ships get to the harbor, they need ME!

'Cause I'm mighty! And I can nudge, bump, butt, shove, ram, push, and pull 'em in. *Here I go.*

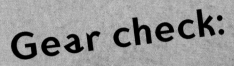

Gear check:

Towropes?	Coiled!
Hull?	Strong!
Bumpers?	Bouncy!
Engines?	Purring!
Propellers?	Whirring!
Stacks?	Smokin'!
Whistle?	

TOOT!

Shipshape
and ready to
TUG!

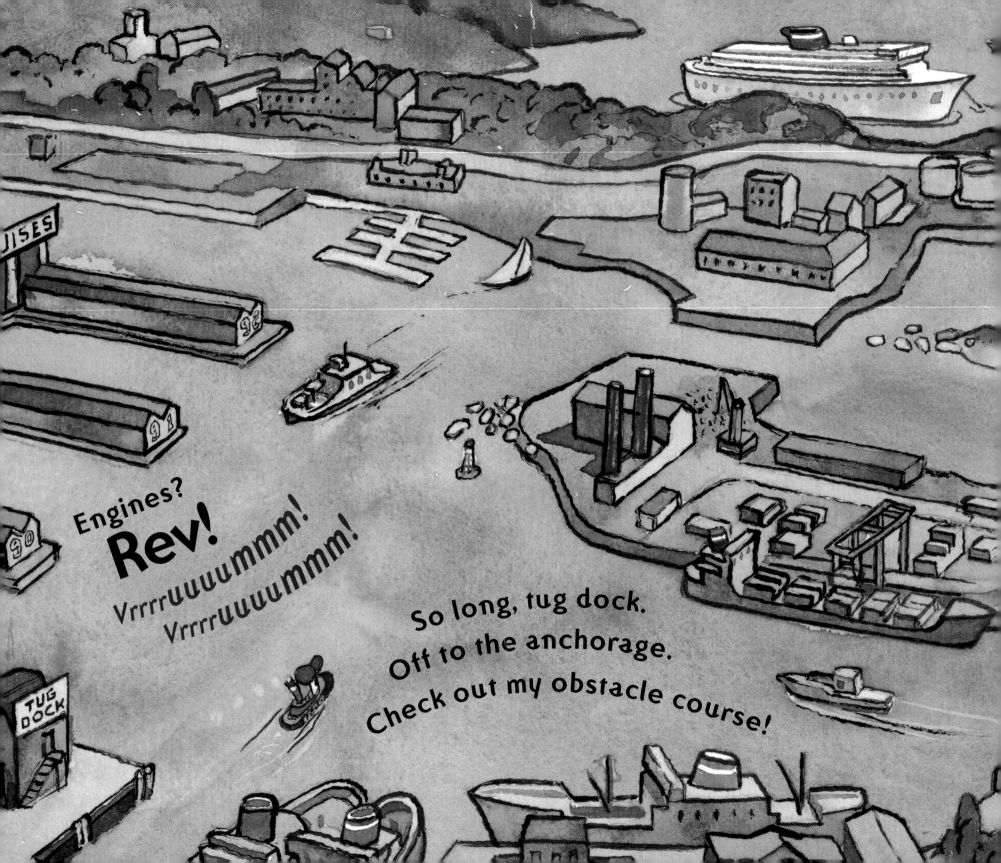

Here's my first tow—
a low-riding tanker
with a belly full of oil.

Tug. Tug. Tug.

Coming in too fast, Moby Dee!
PUTTING ON THE BRAKES.

Engines? **Reverse!**
Mmm**uuuurrrrv!**
Mmm**uuuurrrrv!**

She's **STOPPED!** Parking? My specialty.

MOBY DEE

Circle to the bow: **BUMP!**

Dog it to the stern: **BUTT!**

Round three—
the **Queen Justine,**
a super-duper cruiser,
as **WIDE** as she is long.

*Think this big mama's
got me beat?*
No way!

TOOT, TOOT!

Wide load coming through!

(Pardon me, *Queenie*.)

Let's **TUG!**

Tug.
Tug.
Tug.

QUEEN JUSTINE

I'm all tuggered out. Back to the barn.

Gear check:

Towropes?	Drying.
Hull?	Dented.
Bumpers?	Bent.
Engines?	Backing.
Propellers?	Slacking.
Stacks?	Empty.
Whistle?	Toot!

Got to get some shut-eye.
'Cause three **REALLY BIG** ships
are coming in the morning.

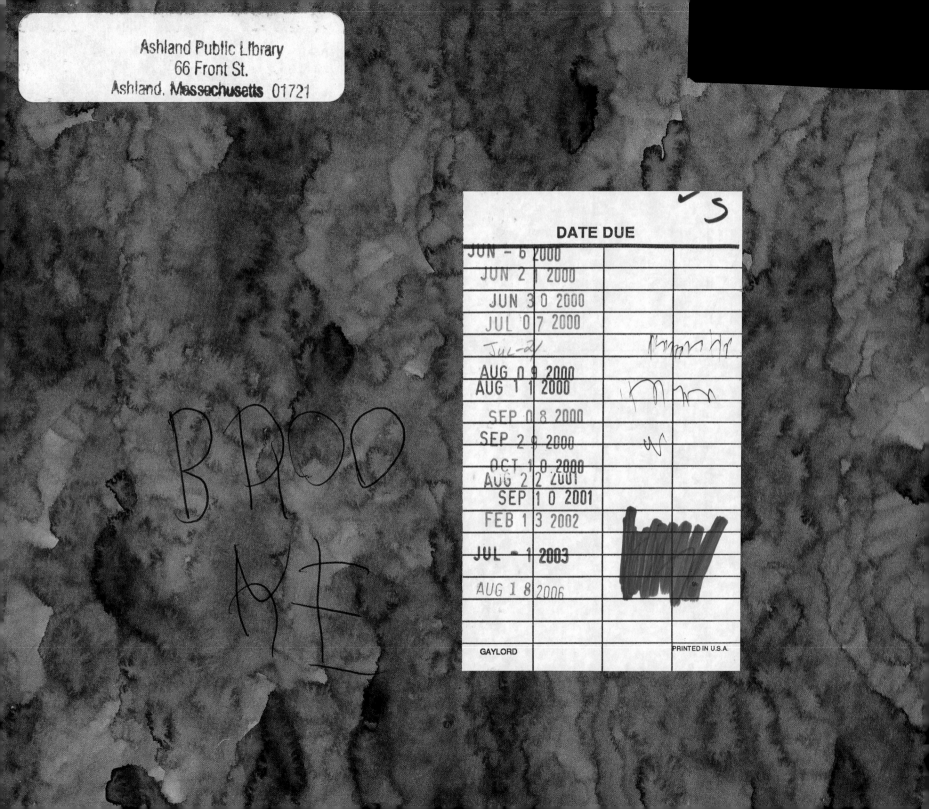

First U.S. edition 1993
First published in Great Britain in 1993 by Walker Books Ltd., London.

Library of Congress Cataloging-in-Publication Data:
Ormerod, Jan
Midnight pillow fight / Jan Ormerod.—1st U.S. ed.
Summary: A young girl engages in a midnight romp with
pillows from around the house.
[1. Pillows—Fiction. 2. Bedtime—Fiction.] I. Title.
PZ7.O634M1 1993   92-53011
[E]–dc20
ISBN 1-56402-169-6

10 9 8 7 6 5 4 3 2 1

Printed and bound in Hong Kong by
Dai Nippon Printing Co. (H.K.) Ltd.

The illustrations in this book are
watercolor and pen and ink.

Candlewick Press
2067 Massachusetts Avenue
Cambridge, Massachusetts 02140